Contents

Acknowledgment: Rebecca Archer for the front cover illustration.

Published by Ladybird Books Ltd
80 Strand London WC2R 0RL
A Penguin Company
15 17 19 20 18 16 14

Printed in Italy

monster stories for under fives

by JOAN STIMSON
illustrated by
GERALD HAWKSLEY

Ladybird

Re-cycled Cyril

Cyril was a round, bouncy monster. He lived with his dad down by the waste tip.

At first the tip made a wonderful home. All day long cars and trucks arrived. They delivered goods which people no longer wanted or needed. Out came old settees, tables, chairs, fridges, television sets and once, even an old trampoline… the very trampoline on which Cyril had learned to bounce!

But Cyril didn't feel bouncy this morning.

"I'm bored, Dad," he complained. "Why is the tip so QUIET these days?"

"Well, son," explained Dad, "it's because people make things last longer or give them away to a good home."

But Cyril wasn't satisfied.

"I want MORE noise and MORE excitement!" he cried.

Suddenly Dad had a brainwave. He squinted up at the calendar.

"We could always have a wash," he said. "We usually have one at this time of year."

Dad pointed to a pink bath with gold taps right at the top of the tip. It was half full of rainwater.

"Oh no!" squealed Cyril. "I'm off!"

As soon as he left the tip, Cyril began to feel bouncy again. There were so many exciting new sights and sounds.

Just along the road he found a sign. "BOTTLE BANK," it said.

"Look at that smart house!" he cried.

Cyril peered up at a large container. It had three Cyril-shaped windows. They were labelled CLEAR, BROWN and GREEN.

"Is anyone at home?" chirped Cyril below the 'green' window.

And, when there was no reply, he bounced right inside.

Very soon Cyril had more noise and excitement than he had ever dreamed of.

All morning people arrived with boxes of empty bottles.

“PING, ZING, TING!” Cyril wasn’t worried about getting hurt because he was a very thick-skinned monster. But he did want to join in the fun.

So Cyril started catching the bottles as they flew in. Then he juggled with them. And, when he'd finished, he flung them against the side of the container.

"Funny," said one lady, "that one took a long time to reach the bottom."

"Must be nearly empty, dear," said her friend.

But the friend was wrong. The bottle bank was almost full. And Cyril was just beginning to feel a little squashed when… *brrmm, brrmm*… a lorry backed up to the container.

"WOW!" cried Cyril. He peered through his little 'green' window. "I'm having a ride."

Brrmm, brrmm! The lorry had arrived at the re-cycling factory, where old bottles are made into new glass.

And, before he knew it, Cyril had been delivered to the first stage of the re-cycling process… the WASHING stage!

"WHOOSH! GASP! SPLUTTER!" Jets of water rained down to soak the labels off the bottles and to make Cyril the cleanest monster ever!

It took a long time for Cyril to scramble home.

"Dad, Dad," he gabbled. "I've been re-cycled!"

Dad squinted down at Cyril and smiled.

"You still look the same to me," said Dad. "You're just cleaner. And so am I," he added proudly. "I've had a wash to celebrate."

Cyril looked puzzled. Dad led him to a smart new sign right by the old pink bath.

"NEW MONSTER FUN PARK," it said. "WORK STARTS TOMORROW."

"WOW!" cried Cyril. He bounced as high as a bottle bank. Then Dad told him about the noisy and exciting rides.

"Are they building all that just for us?" asked Cyril.

Dad shook his head and smiled. "I don't expect so, son," he replied, "but I'm sure they won't mind if WE JOIN IN THE FUN!"

Maisie and the monster show

Mr Marvel was choosing the acts for his Monster Show and all the young monsters were over-excited.

"Please, Mr Marvel," piped up Maisie. "I want to be in the Show too."

Mr Marvel looked down at the little monster.

"All right," he sighed. "Let's see what you can do."

With a delighted squeal, Maisie leaped to join the dancers. She knew the steps by heart. But Maisie was TOO SMALL. She kept tripping up the other monsters.

"Hey!" shrieked the dancers. "Maisie's messing up our act."

"All right, all right! Keep your horns on!" cried Mr Marvel. "Maisie can try something else."

The dancers glided away to slap on some more make-up and Maisie began to recite a rhyme.

It was a very funny rhyme, which Maisie had made up herself. But, although she was word-perfect, Mr Marvel could barely hear her.

"It's no good, Maisie," he cried. "Your voice is TOO SQUEAKY. The mums and dads will never hear you."

"They'll hear ME all right," bellowed a budding comedian.

He barged past Maisie and began to tell a DREADFUL joke.

All afternoon Maisie had to watch bigger and noisier monsters showing off.

"Please, Mr Marvel," she squeaked at the end of rehearsals, "watch me stand on my head."

"Now don't be silly, Maisie," sighed Mr Marvel. "We all know that monsters CAN'T stand on their heads."

"Of course not!" boomed an eager acrobat. "Our horns get in the way."

And with that he pushed Maisie aside and turned TEN cartwheels.

"I know," said Mr Marvel suddenly. "Maisie can take round the snacks in the interval."

That night Maisie squeaked extra loudly on Dad's lap.

"I'm TOO SMALL and TOO SQUEAKY to be in the Monster Show. All I can do is take round the snacks."

It took Dad a long time to persuade Maisie to go to the Show. When they arrived, the dancers were in a panic and Mr Marvel was in a bad temper.

"Just look at them!" he cried. "They've been slapping on TOO MUCH make-up and it's made them come out in spots!"

Maisie scratched her horns and tried not to laugh.

"I know!" she squeaked. "The dancers can tie big hankies round their faces… just like veils. It will make them look mysterious… and hide their spots!"

Maisie went backstage to help to dress the dancers and Mr Marvel announced the beginning of the Show.

"Maisie, Maisie," croaked a voice beside her, "I'm all hoarse. I won't be able to tell my WONDERFUL jokes."

Maisie peered at the budding comedian and tried not to look relieved.

"I know!" she squeaked. "You'll have to MIME your act."

The budding comedian listened carefully and Maisie explained how he could pretend he was learning to ride a bike… with NO WORDS.

The mums and dads loved the dancers in their 'veils'. They rolled in their seats as the comedian tried to ride his imaginary bike. By the interval things were going so smoothly that Maisie actually ENJOYED taking round the snacks.

Everyone settled down for the second half of the Show. Maisie helped the magician to find his rabbit. She rescued a marble from down the musician's trumpet. Then, all too soon, it was time for the last and most exciting act.

"And now…" cried Mr Marvel. There was a terrific roll of drums. "Archie the Acrobat will turn a tantalising TWENTY cartwheels!"

"OOOOH!" cried the mums and dads.

"OOOOH! AAAAGH!" groaned Archie. He'd pulled a muscle and couldn't move!

Maisie heard the groans and bounded onto the stage. She smoothed down her horns and squeaked up at Mr Marvel.

"And now, er…" Mr Marvel began again. He sounded nervous. "The AMAZING MAISIE will… STAND ON HER HEAD!"

"No! Impossible! Can't be done!" exclaimed the mums and dads.

"I'm ninety and never seen it," gasped a Granny monster.

But they were ALL wrong, because that's EXACTLY what the little monster did. And from then on, whenever Mr Marvel had a Monster Show, he never failed to include Maisie!

Not a well monster

I'm not a well monster,
I'm hardly green at all.
My horns are weak and wobbly,
Instead of standing tall.

My warts are pale and pasty,
My hair is almost CLEAN.
One sleepy eye is drooping
And two have lost their gleam.

I think I need a doctor –
My tail's all limp and thin.
I've said goodbye for ever
To whiskers on my chin.

HOORAY! Here comes the medicine –
It's wriggling on my plate.
I'll soon be well again
And I can hardly wait!

Jittery Ginger

Ginger was the jitteriest monster in the whole neighbourhood.

She didn't like the dark. She ran a mile if she saw a spider. But what scared Ginger more than anything else was the thought of children… HUMAN children!

Each night Mum said the same thing. "I can't understand why you're so jittery, Ginger."

She turned on the night-light and read Ginger a monster story. Then she went downstairs.

Mum was just sitting down to a nice hot cup of monster brew, when there was a shriek from upstairs.

“Mum, Mum, there’s a CHILD in my wardrobe!”

Mum rushed upstairs and flung open the wardrobe door.

“Oh Ginger!” she grumbled. “There’s nothing in the wardrobe but monster clothes and toys.”

Mum decided to have an early night. She was just settling down with a good book, when there was a scream from across the landing.

"Mum, Mum, I've had a TERRIBLE nightmare! All about a little girl… with two blue eyes and a yellow ponytail."

"Oh Ginger!" groaned Mum. "How many more times must I tell you? There are no children in THIS neighbourhood."

Mum climbed into bed with Ginger. She was just snuggling down for a good snore when Ginger began to jitter.

"Wake up, Ginger!" cried Mum. "You're having another nightmare."

“It was AWFUL, Mum,” wailed Ginger. “There was a small boy… with rosy cheeks and a tooth missing.”

“Oh Ginger!” growled Mum. “I wish you would understand that there’s NOTHING scary about children.”

Next morning Mum was up early. “Come on, Ginger,” she yawned. “We’re going on a journey.”

By the time they arrived it was lunchtime. Mum and Ginger sat by the roadside and ate their monsterbuns.

"This way," said Mum, when they'd finished. She took Ginger across the road and held her up to some railings.

Ginger looked over the railings and gaped.

"It's a school playground," explained Mum. "The children are having their playtime."

Ginger couldn't take her eyes away from the children. Running, whooping, squealing, hurtling, hiding or simply eating their sandwiches, they filled the playground.

"Mum, Mum!" cried Ginger in an excited whisper. "Those children aren't scary at all. They're doing just the same things as I do!"

From then on Ginger slept like a top. She gave away her night-light. She had the best collection of spiders in the neighbourhood. And on her very next birthday Ginger asked for a doll… WITH TWO BLUE EYES AND A YELLOW PONYTAIL!

Night of the dinosaurs

"I WISH there still were dinosaurs!" said Danny. He said it every day!

It had all started when Danny was tiny. His parents had taken him to a museum and Danny had been mad about dinosaurs ever since.

By the time he went to school, Danny was a dinosaur expert. At first Miss Fletcher was pleased. But then she became impatient because Danny ALWAYS said the same thing: "I WISH there still were dinosaurs!"

One day Danny's class went on a trip to the zoo. The children rushed eagerly from one animal to the next… all except Danny.

At the end of the trip Danny's friend Nancy made a special speech to the zookeeper. But halfway through there was a loud wail:
"I WISH there still were dinosaurs!"

"Be QUIET, Danny!" cried Miss Fletcher.

Nancy was furious. She'd spent ages practising her speech and now Danny had spoiled it.

That night Danny's parents were going to a party. Danny was going to sleep at Nancy's... in a tent! When he arrived, there was a note waiting for him:

Dear Danny,
There still ARE dinosaurs!
We live in Nancy's garden.
Tony Tyrannosaurus
Dave Diplodocus
Stephanie Stegosaurus

"WOW!" cried Danny, and clambered into the tent.

"Nightie-night," said Nancy. "Don't let the dinosaurs bite!"

"Whatever do you mean?" cried Danny. He'd never slept in a tent before and he was beginning to feel nervous.

But Nancy was already snoring.

Danny couldn't stop thinking about the note. His last thought before he dropped off to sleep was: "I WISH there still were dinosaurs... BUT NOT AT NIGHT!"

Suddenly something moved and Danny woke up in a panic. "Nancy!" he cried.

But Nancy had disappeared. Danny could just read the note on her pillow.

Dear Danny,
We've got Nancy. Now
we're coming for you!
Tony Tyrannosaurus
Dave Diplodocus
Stephanie Stegosaurus

Slowly, very slowly, Danny opened the tent flap. He peered into the darkness. And then he saw it… a terrible tyrannosaurus!

"T-T-Tony," he croaked, "have you got Nancy?"

There was no answer. Then Danny looked closer and saw that the tyrannosaurus was just a row of bushes.

"Phew!" cried Danny. Then he added bravely. "I WISH there still were dinosaurs… BUT NOT IN NANCY'S GARDEN."

Suddenly something rustled. Danny turned and saw an enormous white shape looming in the moonlight. It was a dreadful diplodocus!

"D-D-Dave," he squeaked, "I'm looking for Nancy."

There was no reply. Then Danny looked closer and saw that the white shape was just clothes hanging on a line.

“Phew!” cried Danny. He was very relieved – but not for long.

Strange noises came from behind the tent. Danny crept round to peek. And then he saw it… a spiky stegosaurus!

"S-S-Stephanie," he squawked, "please give back Nancy."

"All right then!" cried a cheerful voice.

You could have knocked Danny down with a dandelion! The stegosaurus was only a garden shed. Its spikes were the funny tiles on the roof. And Nancy was standing in the doorway!

"*I* wrote those notes," she said, "because YOU spoiled my speech."

Danny and Nancy lay awake for a long time. Danny didn't feel like talking about dinosaurs, so Nancy told him all about the things he'd been missing. And just before they fell asleep, she recited her zoo speech… right to the end.

The next day at school, Miss Fletcher was still cross. She hadn't forgotten that Danny had been rude to the zookeeper. "And what do you have to say for yourself, Danny?" she said.

Danny stood up. He took a deep breath.

"I WISH," he began, "I wish that I could go swimming and hiking and learn judo and ice skating and play football and make new friends. And most of all I wish that next time we go to the zoo… that *I* could make the speech to the zookeeper."

"Good heavens!" cried Miss Fletcher. "But what about dinosaurs?"

"Dinosaurs," said Danny firmly, "are a thing of the past… AND BELONG IN MUSEUMS!"

The cheerful dinosaur

One day a cheerful dinosaur
Came knocking at my door.
"I want to see your house," she said.
"I'd like a guided tour."

I took her to the kitchen,
She ate up all the food.
"And now I want to play," she said,
"I'm in a playful mood."

I took her to my bedroom,
She bounced onto the bed.
"I've made a dent up there," she said,
"But didn't hurt my head."

I took her to the garden,
She stopped to stroke the cat.
"I'd like to try your bike," she said,
But then she squashed it flat.

She trampled on the flowers,
She broke my brother's swing.
"I've never had such fun," she said,
"You ARE a friendly thing!

"I'll bring MY friends tomorrow,
Just six or eight or ten."
But then, thank goodness, I woke up!
And all was calm again.